I0733324

REMAINS OF CHRISTMAS

A TWISTED CHRISTMAS SHORT STORY

ALEXANDRIA BLAELOCK

BlueMere Books
MELBOURNE, AUSTRALIA

Publisher's Note: This is a work of fiction. Names, characters, places, and incidents are a product of the author's imagination. Locations and public names are sometimes used for atmospheric purposes. Any resemblance to actual people, living or dead, or to businesses, companies, events, institutions, or locations is completely coincidental.

Copyright © 2021 Alexandria Blaelock.

All rights reserved. No part of this publication may be reproduced, distributed or transmitted in any form or by any means, including photocopying, recording, or other electronic or mechanical methods, without the prior written permission of the publisher, except in the case of brief quotations embodied in critical reviews and certain other non-commercial uses permitted by copyright law.

For permission requests, please contact enquiries@bluemerebooks.com.

Ordering Information:
Discounts are available on quantity purchases. For details, contact orders@bluemerebooks.com.

Remains of Christmas/Alexandria Blaelock
paperback ISBN: 978-1-925749-95-3
digital ISBN: 978-1-925749-96-0

BlueMere Books
www.bluemerebooks.com

REMAINS OF CHRISTMAS

I loved Christmas when I was young, for as far back as I can remember.

When I was a child, it was all about Dad.

He was in service, but rather than following him from base to base like other military families, Mother insisted the rest of us stay in one place.

"I want to live like a normal family," she declared.

And so, the rest of us did.

But then I suppose, hers was a farming family, not military. Her roots were buried deep in the soil for a hundred generations.

Such a stereotype to fall in love with a boy from the base, especially as she'd made it a rule to avoid them.

Though having seen pictures of him when he was younger, I can understand that.

I would have gone for him too, straight and true as an arrow.

Mother had pinned her hopes on marrying a farmer from one of the neighbouring towns, and by the time she realised Dad was from the base, not another town, it was too late.

She was sweet on him.

It's another cliché that the heart wants what the heart wants, but it was certainly true for her.

Dad moved from base to base as the years passed, but without fail, he came home in mid-December and stayed for four weeks before shipping out again.

And every time he left she was pregnant again.

I thought an annual baby was normal.

When I was older, I heard a joke about a couple having sex once a year and suddenly it clicked - it wasn't just that Mother was very good at catching the stork's attention as it flew over.

I guess no one bothered with that joke about our family, because her annual cycle was so obvious.

So in anticipation, our preparations for Christmas usually started late September with getting the Christmas puddings ready.

For weeks our house would smell of dried fruits steeping in brandy, and then a little later, as the puddings were mixed and cooked, of cinnamon, cloves and sweet treacly cooked sugar.

Later still, they'd sit in the larder, gently perfuming the air as they intensified in flavour.

Makes my mouth water just thinking about it, though I've never made a pudding myself.

I suppose pudding making is a lost domestic art, though perhaps someone somewhere continues the tradition.

As September gave way to October, the attention focused on preparing the house for Dad's arrival.

Unlike other women who leave the household maintenance to their husbands, Mother wanted to gift him the opportunity to fully relax at home.

And presumably take care of her.

Ahem.

So, during October and November, she started going through the house room by room; sweeping, cleaning and painting.

We'd come home from school, never knowing when it was our room's turn and we'd have to sleep on a pile of blankets on the floor.

I can't imagine what a winter Christmas would be like, but thank goodness ours falls over Summer and we could leave the windows open to let the smell of fresh paint out.

And cook outside to prevent the smell settling into the clean house.

As November gave way to December, we would reach fever pitch.

The paint would be clean and dry. The house spic and span. And we would be fully occupied with cleaning the old Christmas decorations and making the new while Mother made stacks of shortbread, gingerbread biscuits, and fruit mince pies.

We'd make huge strings of popcorn, though I still don't understand the purpose of them. Aside from tasks to keep us occupied during the school holidays, and snacks for times when our parents had "things" to do.

And then chains made from slips of paper glued end-to-end.

Scavenging pine cones from around the farm and painting them white, silver and gold.

Sticks bent into star shapes and wrapped with twine. Weaving scraps of fabric into heart shapes.

And then one day, out of the blue, Gunnery Sergeant Philip James Craddock would come walking up the long farm drive, blue uniform jacket hanging open, with his duffel bag slung over his shoulder.

When it was my turn, I realised she always knew when he was coming, because Aunty Allison who owned the town beauty salon would visit the house that morning.

But for us, it was on.

Racing down the drive to be the first to meet him, and be folded into his enormous hug.

I don't know how Mother could stand on the porch waiting for him.

Perhaps the knowledge the night was hers helped. And with that in mind, they did their very best to exhaust us so we went to bed early.

The next day, was the only day of the year Mother could sleep in.

Or perhaps *wanted* to sleep in.

Dad would creep out of bed early and cook us a "military" breakfast of sausage, beans and eggs.

And then he'd take us all out across the farm looking for the best Christmas tree.

Even the baby.

And he would keep us out all day, stopping for a picnic lunch of sandwiches and homemade orange cordial he'd prepared earlier.

Exhausted, happy and triumphant, we'd come home late in the day to put the tree up and decorate it, along with the house.

And that evening, after dinner, we'd sit outside on the verandah and eat the first of the Christmas puddings, with rich creamy custard.

Somehow Dad would always get the threepenny bit, and he would look at his children ranged around him with pride, and flick it into the air above us.

And somehow, it would always be me that caught it.

Looking back, those days were truly magical.

The sun was always shining, the days were always balmy and warm, and mosquitoes never bit.

But isn't childhood always glorious when you look back?

Then one year, Dad didn't come walking up the drive.

Two officers, a man and a woman, arrived in a staff car instead.

They took their hats off when they saw Mother standing on the verandah.

Something strange was going on, and we clustered restlessly together nearby to watch.

They saluted her at the foot of the stairs, with a smart, precisely timed swing of their arms. Then walked up to the house and offered her an envelope. Something was said, and she nodded.

They walked back down the stairs, turned back to face her, offering another salute before they climbed into the car and drove away.

It seemed to me they sought me out among the bunch of us.

I was watching them so intently I didn't see her fall, nor the rest of my siblings flock to her side.

It took my eldest brother several shouts to attract my attention and send me running helter-skelter through the wheat fields for Grandmother.

Shortly after that, it was no real surprise to anyone in my extended family that I announced my intention to attend the Military Academy.

I had not been able to shake the memory of those officers, driving that car, saluting Mother in their deepest of deep blue uniforms topped with the striking silver braiding.

The neat efficiency and synchronicity of their movements.

The perfect precision of their haircuts.

More importantly, their sleek, well-fed bodies.

As we stood on the train station, the train huffing and puffing in its eagerness to leave, Mother hugged me tightly and said, "I wish it wasn't you of all my children."

My eldest brother said she stood waving, long after the train had disappeared from sight.

But I had left the farm without looking back. For me, life was just beginning, and I was looking forward to it.

I remember the day I arrived at the Academy, its grey stone walls looming above me. Some say it looks more like a prison, but I loved the way its tall brutal buildings assaulted the sky.

I loved its lush green sports ovals and parade grounds, the formal gravel drives and pathways leading directly from one building to another, and the way it was built into the cliffs surrounding it.

Manifestly defensible.

But even more than that, I loved the statue of the mounted hussar in the main forecourt.

Leaning forward, sword drawn, charging towards the main gate as though challenging each and every person to sought entry.

As if it knew who was worthy and who was not.

I cannot have been the only one who stood taller and straighter in the face of his challenge.

I remember meeting the Recruit Sergeant the first time, and the height his eyebrows achieved when I loudly announced myself "Cadet Penelope June Craddock, reporting for duty."

He almost took a step back to get a better look at me. Something I noticed as I met each of the Officers who undertook student training.

And for a short time after graduating into the forces.

And the reason for this was that Dad had been an Academy legend in his time.

Top of every single class.

Decent margins between him and the next in Military Strategy and Military History.

Time trial wins on the cross-country runs up the mountain, and down to the bay.

And Captain of the winning team in the final battle simulation.

It was a lot to live up to, but I made up my mind I was going to beat every single one of his records.

I wanted to win against everyone, and graduate as the most successful candidate ever.

Of course, it was hard having grown up on a farm instead of a base.

But I pursued my goal with intense focus; accompanied by no one, excepting a photo of Dad I'd carefully cut out of an old yearbook in the library with my hideously sharp penknife.

While the other kids were meeting up and getting drunk on the top of the administration building, I was in the wilds, running like there was no tomorrow.

And when they were getting drunk down on the beach hidden by a fold in the cliffs, I was practising drills on my own.

And when they were getting drunk up on the mountain in a disused powder magazine, I was studying in my room.

Christmas that first year, I had written to my eldest brother, telling him when I would arrive, and asking him to keep it a secret from Mother.

I walked from the train station, and up the long farm drive, grey cadet uniform hanging open, with my duffel bag slung over my shoulder.

It felt to me as though Dad's spirit had been lost, found me at the Academy, and followed me home.

Neither Mother nor my siblings had any idea I was coming.

Except the eldest of course, and he had somehow got them all in the yard doing stuff as I approached.

It was so wonderful to see them; as if I'd picked up my longing for home and family at the gate where I'd left it on my way out.

I could see them milling about, in confusion, not knowing who I was.

Mother figured it out first, and as she ran lightly down the steps and out onto the drive, she picked up speed.

I dropped my duffel and braced myself as she ran into my hug.

And after a moment, the smallest children who barely remembered me after a year's absence ran after Mother, and gradually the elder siblings figured it out and proceeded toward me at a more leisurely pace.

Until I was in the centre of a rugby scrum of hugging.

Even after my siblings let go and moved back, Mother remained clinging like a barnacle.

I didn't mean to take over Dad's role at Christmas; it was just that my internal clock had moved to Morning Watch while I was at the Academy - I'd needed the extra hours to study.

So as I got up and tip-toed to the kitchen to make myself coffee, planning to go out into the farm until everyone else was awake, my siblings joined me one by one.

Expecting what they thought was a typical "military" breakfast of sausage, beans and eggs.

But which I knew by then was all that Dad could cook.

I didn't want to disappoint them, so I made breakfast. Only *I* left a plate wrapped in foil on a very low heat in the oven for Mother, and made my siblings wash the dishes and clean up the kitchen.

While they did that, I got the youngest up, and left a note propped on the coffee pot to let Mother know the kids were fine with me and hadn't been kidnapped.

And we went out to do what we had always done, venture out across the farm to find the best Christmas tree.

One of the others had prepared sandwiches and homemade orange cordial, so the whole flock of us stayed out all day.

Returning exhausted, happy and triumphant, to put the tree up and decorate it, along with the house.

Regardless of whatever else Mother thought about me taking the siblings out, she prepared the last of the year before's Christmas puddings.

And after dinner, we sat on the verandah and ate it with rich creamy custard.

My eldest brother tucked a bright, shiny threepenny bit into my hand. I looked around at Mother and my siblings, then flicked it into the air above them.

As if time had slowed down, it spun end-over-end and landed in the skirts of the youngest of them. I glanced at my eldest brother, and he nodded, just once, with satisfaction.

And so in this way, the pattern for the next five years of my education were set.

I wish I could say how happy I was to graduate with honours, beating every single one of my classmates, and Dad's records.

Even if I only made one true friend in all that time.

But the so-called War of Independence broke out, and we cadets were sent out to defend the country without even their qualifying ranks to protect them.

I left without looking back.

Instead of the expected analysis role, my first deployment was in command of a small fighting unit.

I'm not ashamed to say I looked at the well-seasoned fighting men, and I as good as shat my pants at the thought of commanding them.

But I was very fortunate to have under my command, a number of men who'd served with Dad.

And I had the good sense to listen to their experience, and plan my plays according to their strengths.

Somehow, we managed to hold our own until December.

It was Christmas that caught us.

Foolishly I'd allowed a ration of brandy that day, because, well, Christmas. And the pudding.

Because we were all tired, bored, and homesick.

And because I thought we were safe in our foxhole; I didn't set reliable sentries.

But for the Empire, Christmas was just another day.

We were the last unit caught by the Empire, and in that way, I'd built my own reputation on the foundation of Dad's strategic military brilliance.

I thought they'd just shoot us, after all, if I'd been in charge, that's would I have done.
Best strategic outcome.

And in any case, they'd bombed the crap out of the country.

Including my childhood home, and all my relatives, evaporated with half the county as a lesson to the rest of us.

For some, the internment camp was a kind of holiday. Conditions weren't bad, the food was good and regular, and many units relaxed their conduct.

Perhaps they'd been so completely demoralised they didn't care anymore. Or perhaps they'd never comported themselves with military dignity.

All captured military personnel have a duty to escape, so I kept my unit focused on planning and working towards an escape.

And well away from the unruly mob we were quartered with.

One day we were called to an assembly in the main quadrangle. I listened with incredulity as they outlined a kind of lottery granting us freedom.

A few of us at a time, to spend some time in isolation and retraining before being released into the community.

The lotteries took place weekly, twenty at a time.

We'd assemble in the quadrangle. They assured us once again that all our names were in the barrel. Then span it round and round, and drew a name. Span it again, and drew someone else.

Like a game show.

After a couple of weeks, I realised that the draws weren't really random.

The people slated for freedom were all highly skilled individuals whose skills could be put to use elsewhere.

Once they'd been deprogrammed.

I pulled the unit together to add this information to the data we already had.

My own Sergeant was surprised it had taken me that long to connect the dots, but he was always a highly suspicious individual.

Well experienced in more personal fields useful to me, but wouldn't get him a ticket out.

The consensus of the unit, was that *when* they called my name, I should leave without a fight.

In the meantime, we'd continue working on the plan and implement it as soon as possible.

But this wasn't the kind of camp you could escape. We all knew that when the list of names ran out, it would be curtains for those left behind.

That Christmas, my name was drawn.

We'd shared a good meal, with a ration of alcohol before the call. It had gone to my head by the time I hugged each of my men and walked towards the guards.

As the gates closed behind me, I heard gunfire break out behind me.

I'd been expecting it, yet my legs still froze for an instant, and my heart skipped a beat before I walked on.

Not looking back.

Vowing that I would somehow find it within me to live a full and active life on my unit's behalf.

That was the last Christmas I celebrated.

I'm old now, and I've lived under the Empire's rule for more than three-quarters of my life.

But sometimes, I still wish I could go back to that day and die a valiant, if ultimately useless death.

Now and again, when I get drunk and maudlin, I wonder if they were the lucky ones to be spared what came next.

Not that life within the Empire has been awful for me, though I'm greeted as a traitor or collaborator by my countrymen, and treated as a spy or terrorist by citizens of the Empire.

And that's kind of okay, I'm used to not being one thing or the other.

But regardless of what people think of me personally, my skills as a senior strategic analyst guarantee me a certain amount of leeway.

More so now that I am so thoroughly inculcated with Empire language and social mores I can barely understand my own people.

It makes me wonder what else I might have got away with in the time before the invasion.

The Empire is highly technological, with many novel gadgets that seemed to me like magic.

The things you can do with your minds.

I suppose I'd never seen a need for most of them. But after a while, I adapted, and it seemed I couldn't live without them.

I looked back on my life and wondered how I had ever survived its simplicity.

It's not that we were naive or simple-minded, but that we were short-sighted and complacent.

That's what ultimately cost us the freedom to freely and proudly proclaim our country's name.

Pure arrogance.

I can't say I blame the Emperor; we were clearly begging to be taken down a peg or two.

Or at least that's what the history books say.

Perhaps it's easier for our younglings this way.

As my generation dies out, the next will be the pure products of the Empire's social structures and educational systems.

As for me, I somehow managed to catch up with the technology and provide the innovative edge the Empire was looking for.

To learn and adapt, as I always had.

It can be a terrible life for a conquered people.

Some went mad and refused to adapt, maintaining their traditional dress and language.

And some threw themselves into the new ways.

But I didn't really *believe* in either.

As I wear my black and gold braided uniform, I am conscious the Emperor is watching.

I have lived a modest life and not drawn attention to myself.

I've kept my mouth shut, and never, until now, wrote, said, or done anything that might draw unwarranted attention or cause suspicion.

Christmas however, has not.

It's spread its unique magic across the Empire, but the original meaning is mostly lost, gone underground and into hiding.

Now it's a unique marketing opportunity beamed directly into people's brains.

Compelling them to buy thoughtless tokens of affection they don't feel, for people they don't like.

For about a decade, I've chosen to deploy over the last quarter of the year.

Every October first, I report for duty.

As I take the lift and descend into the shielded basement, the advertising fades and disappears, leaving me with a blissfully empty mind.

Free to think my own thoughts and feel my own emotions and physical sensations, not the implanted ones.

Three blissful months, followed by one more of gradually increasing intensity until the advertising is back to full blast on the first of February.

Some young people like you find it hard to adjust to being alone inside your own head, not all of you can take it.

But you must learn to adapt, to fine-tune your focus; your intelligence work depends on your ability to tune into the nuances.

If you can't, or won't adjust, you'll be sent back to the surface.

Perhaps you'll recover your mind when you get there.

Or perhaps you won't.

Perhaps you'll become one of the "zombies", chained together, sweeping paths in the Imperial

Gardens, trapped and unable to escape the silence.

Objects of derision.

Forever.

You've done well to get this far.

I will leave you to the next phase of your training; a Watch's worth of the shielding simulation.

《《 • 》》

As I closed the door on the recruits, I took a deep breath and let it out.

We lost a couple every session, but it was better to weed them out *before* we started training them to do their actual jobs.

I went back to the control room where my new adjutant had the monitors running and recording.

"Do many recruits report you?"

I smiled at him warmly, "only the exceptional ones like you." I didn't tell him it was part of the testing - those who didn't were weeded out by the end of the quarter.

"And is it true you enjoy the adblocker? The privacy of your own thoughts?"

As a person born in the Empire, he'd been implanted as a baby. Had never known anything other than the conditioning.

"My implant was never turned on."

He sucked in a gasp.

"It was enough for the Emperor that I submitted to the surgery."

I didn't need to tell him that the risk of implanting as an adult was very great. If it hadn't worked, *I* would have been one of the brainless working in the Imperial Gardens.

But I was a soldier, and my job was to fight. It didn't much matter to me who for.

What could I possibly have done if not this? Perhaps not for the reasons my unit might have expected, but I lived.

I'd gone through *a* surgery, but I wasn't convinced an implant had been installed.

The thing about conditioning your population from birth, is that they don't have an opinion between them. They're just drones.

For the Emperor, the only realistic option for generating new ideas is conquering other nations.

And as the commander of the last unit captured, the potential loss of my strategic mind may have been too high a price for him to countenance.

So, if my adjunct played his cards right, he could well have his turned off in ten or twenty years.

Something only granted to those with potential.

And the thing about Christmas was that it gave the populace a focus it didn't have before.

A sanitised one of course.

Wouldn't want them getting any ideas.

THE END

ABOUT THE AUTHOR

Alexandria Blaelock writes stories, some of them for *Ellery Queen's Mystery Magazine* and *Pulphouse Fiction Magazine*. She's also written five self-help books applying business techniques to personal matters like getting dressed, cleaning house, and feeding your friends.

As a recovering Project Manager, she's probably too fond of sticking to plan. She lives in a forest because she enjoys birdsong, the scent of gum leaves and the sun on her face. When not telecommuting to parallel universes from her Melbourne based imagination, she watches K-dramas, talks to animals, and drinks Campari. At the same time.

Discover more at www.alexandriablaelock.com.

BOOKS BY
ALEXANDRIA BLAELOCK

SHORT STORY COLLECTIONS

The Histories of Hayward Hall
Lovelorn, Lovestruck and Love at First Sight
Common or Garden Variety Heroes
Case Files of the Wilkinson Detective Agency
Unavoidable Fates
Christmas Travesties

OTHER FICTION

That Love Nonsense

MS BLAELOCK'S BOOKS

Stress Free Dinner Parties
Signature Wardrobe Planning
Holistic Personal Finance
Minimally Viable Housekeeping
Planning a Life Worth Living

SELECTED SHORT STORIES

Alma's Grace
Balancing the Book
Carmelita Basingstoke
Fate in Your Hands
Kiss of Death
Lady of the Looking Glass
Life in the Security Directorate
Long Weekend in the Snow
Love in the Past Tense
Love in the Security Directorate
Morning Star, Evening Star, Superstar
Needy Bitch
Payton's Run
Phoenix Child
Secret Singer
Shining Star
Ship in a Bottle
Simone Says Hands in the Air
Special Relativity in Space
The Bygone Boyfriend
The Day the Schedule Broke
The Ghost Detectors
The Guardian's Vigil
The Mince Pie Mystery
The Mystery of the Master Suite
The Pseudonym's Bride
The Shadow Thieves
The Time-Space Paradox
Toy Soldiers

www.ingramcontent.com/pod-product-compliance
Lightning Source LLC
Chambersburg PA
CBHW062003190726

48285CB00003BA/1176